BEST STORIES

FOR

SEVEN YEAR OLDS

BY VIVIEN ALCOCK

STEPHEN ELBOZ

ELIZABETH LAIRD

SHARON CREECH

AND JOAN AIKEN

Illustrated by Anthony Lewis

Pigeon Talk © Vivien Alcock 1995
The Bear © Stephen Elboz 1995
The Cowboy of Paradise Farm © Elizabeth Laird 1995
The Gift © Sharon Creech 1995
The Mysterious Meadow © Joan Aiken 1995

This collection © Hodder Children's Books 1995
Illustrations © Anthony Lewis 1995

First published in Great Britain in 1995 by
Hodder Children's Books

A Catalogue record for this book is available from the British
Library

ISBN 0340 646357

Typeset by
Avon Dataset Ltd, Bidford on Avon, Warwickshire B50 4JH

Printed and bound in Great Britain by
Cox & Wyman Ltd, Reading, Berks.

Hodder Children's Books
A Division of Hodder Headline plc
338 Euston Road
London NW1 3BH

CONTENTS

Pigeon Talk

Vivien Alcock

Pigeon Talk

Vivien Alcock

The corner house was half hidden by low fruit trees and rickety fences. Hundreds of pigeons sat on the roof and on the branches of the apple trees, murmuring softly to one another.

"Cu-cu-*coo-oo*, cu-cu-*coo-oo*."

Jessie Brown loved to hear them. The children passed the house on their way to school. At least, her sister Alice and the

Hudson boys, Robert and Tim, passed it without a glance. But Jessie always stopped.

It made Alice cross.

"Don't lag behind!" she'd yell. "You're such a baby! Mum told me to look after you and how can I, if you're not there?"

"I only wanted to look at the pigeons," Jessie said.

Robert, a sturdy boy, with fat red cheeks, told her it was dangerous to stand there.

"Why?"

"Because the pigeons will splat on you," he said, sniggering. Alice told him not to be rude.

That night, when Jessie and her sister were in their room, getting ready for bed, Alice said, "You know that house with the pigeons, Jessie? Who do you think lives there?"

"I don't know." Jessie had never seen anyone come out of the faded blue door. When she'd peeped through the chinks in the fence, she'd never seen anyone in the garden. Only pigeons, pecking in the grass.

"Who lives there?" she asked.

"A wicked witch," Alice said.

Jessie sniffed. Her older sister had a face like an angel's but Jessie knew she often told lies. Like the time she'd told Jessie that Mr Hudson next door was a vampire who turned into a bat at night and slept hanging upside down from the light fitting.

"If he calls here, don't let him in," she'd said, "or he'll drink our blood."

So the next time Mr Hudson had called at their house to borrow some milk, Jessie had screamed and slammed the door in his face. It had been very difficult to explain this to her parents. One look at Alice's face had warned her not to mention vampires, so she'd said she'd mistaken him for a burglar. Dad had told her not to be so silly. "You've known Mr Hudson for years," he'd said. Alice had winked at her.

I'll never believe anything she tells me ever again, Jessie had thought.

Now, remembering this and other similar occassions, she said calmly, "Witches have cats, not pigeons."

"Ah," Alice said, "You don't know everything." She settled herself comfortably on the foot of Jessie's bed. "This witch did have a cat once called Perloma. But one day some bad children threw stones at it and chased it away and it never came back. In revenge, she changed them all into pigeons. Haven't you ever wondered why they never sit on any of the other houses in Rimm Hill? Only on hers. It's because they hope one day she'll relent and change them back."

It couldn't be true and yet – Jessie had seen the pigeons circling in the sky, and coming back, always coming back to that one house. The house with the apple trees and the blue door. But she said stubbornly, "I don't believe you. Witches turn people into frogs and toads. Why does *she* turn them into pigeons?"

Alice leaned towards her and licked her lips. "Because she likes pigeon pie," she whispered. "She feeds them, she fattens them, then she cooks them in a pie."

"I don't believe you," Jessie said again.

But that night she dreamed she was a pigeon sitting on the roof of the house in Rimm Hill. And all the other pigeons crowded round her, murmuring mournfully.

"She'll cook you *too-ooo*, cook you *too-ooo*."

The next day was bright and hot. Jessie told herself that dreams were only dreams and Alice was a mean liar and there were no such things as witches. But as they came towards

6

the house, she could hear the low purring of the birds, and they still seemed to say,

"Cook you *too-oo*, cook you *too-oo*."

"No, you won't!" she muttered.

Tim Hudson looked at her. He was younger than his brother, a small, quiet boy, timid as a mouse. He never spoke to her, though he sometimes smiled. Perhaps he was shy. Perhaps the cat had got his tongue.

"Do you know who lives in this house, Tim?" she asked.

"A wicked witch," he said, "that's what they say. Do you believe in witches?"

"No. Do you?"

"No. No, I don't," he said, but he didn't sound too sure.

They had stopped and were looking over the gate towards the blue front door. Parked against the wall beside it was an old-fashioned broomstick, a bundle of twigs tied round the end of a pole.

"Look!" Jessie cried. "A witch's broomstick!"

As they stared at it, they heard the sound of a bolt being drawn, and the doorhandle began to turn.

"Quick!" Tim cried, and they fled after Alice and Robert who were some way ahead.

"Are you sure you don't believe in witches?" Jessie whispered to him when she'd recovered her breath.

"Are you sure *you* don't?" he retorted, and they smiled sheepishly at one another.

After that, they often walked together, lagging a little behind Alice and Robert. At first they hurried past the house with the pigeons but after a week or two they became bolder and would stop and stare. They never saw the witch, if a witch she was. They sometimes waved in case she was hiding behind her curtains but there was no answering wave. And the pigeons sat on the roof and in the trees, watching them and murmuring to one another.

"What do you think the pigeons are saying?" Jessie asked Tim.

"Pigeons can't talk," he told her, laughing. "They only know one word – Coo. It's hardly enough for a conversation."

A week later, on their way back from school, they saw the pigeons fluttering around the house in an odd, disorganised way. Alice and Robert didn't notice and walked on. But Jessie stopped, puzzled, for the birds were making odd unfamiliar noises. "What's the matter with them?" she said. "Has something frightened them?"

"A cat, I expect. Look out! Here they come!" Tim cried.

The pigeons were all around them now. They flew so close that the children could feel the wind of their wings fanning their cheeks, and see the frantic expressions in their small round eyes.

"They're trying to tell us something," Jessie said, "but I can't make it out."

"Perhaps they're hungry. Perhaps nobody's fed them today."

"Do you think the witch is dead?" Jessie asked.

"I don't know. She could be ill."

"I'd better go and see," Jessie said, for the pigeons were now flying into the garden and it seemed to her that they were calling her,

"C-come *too-oo*, you *too-oo!*"

"Jessie, wait! Supposing it's a trap?" Tim cried, but she was already through the gate and out of sight round the side of the house. He ran after her, shouting, "Jessie, come back! Come back!"

Robert and Alice, some way ahead, heard him and turned. "Where are the kids?" Alice demanded, suddenly frightened. "I can't see them. Where have they gone?"

Jessie and Tim were in the witch's garden. As they came through the apple trees, pigeons exploded from the ground. At first they could only see wings, pale feathers flying, dazzling their eyes. Then, as the birds settled in the trees, they saw a fat woman in a flowered dress lying in the middle of a small shaggy lawn.

"The witch!" Tim whispered.

She was not dead. They could hear her harsh snoring breath above the sound of the birds. She was lying on her back, her plump face oddly distorted, her eyes wide open and staring.

"Go next door and ask them to ring for an ambulance," Jessie said. "Tell them she's had a fit or something. Quick, Tim."

He ran off without arguing.

Jessie sat on the grass beside the old lady. Or the witch, if a witch she was. "You'll be all right," she told her, for the woman's eyes looked frightened. "The ambulance will be here in a minute. Don't worry."

The old lady seemed to be trying to say something but could only grunt. Her brown eyes turned sideways and then looked back at Jessie. Then sideways again and back.

"What is it?" Jessie asked.

The woman flapped her hand over, palm upwards on the grass. A pigeon hopped onto it, as if hoping for food. Jessie gently pushed it away.

"Are you worried about your pigeons?" she asked. "We'll look after them, if you like. We'll feed them for you, me and Tim." She felt the fingers tighten a little and then relax. The brown eyes looked happier.

Jessie sat in the peaceful garden, holding the old lady's hand, and listening to the sound of the pigeons talking. She heard quite clearly what they were saying.

Then everyone came running, scattering the birds into the sky. First it was Alice and Robert, then Tim and the next-door neighbour who told them the ambulance was on its way and wrapped a warm blanket round the old lady. Then the ambulance came singing down the road. The old lady was lifted gently onto a stretcher and carried out to where the ambulance waited, with its doors open.

"Is she your gran?" one of the paramedics asked Jessie.

"No," she said. "Me and Tim, we're her friends. We're going to feed her pigeons for her."

The man smiled and told her the old lady was going to be all right. "She's lucky to have such good friends," he said before he shut the door and the ambulance moved off.

Everyone was pleased with her and Tim.

Mum and Dad, when they heard about it, said they'd been splendid, noticing something was wrong and calling for help so quickly. Even Alice seemed impressed.

That night, she sat on the foot of Jessie's bed. "It was very brave of you to go into her garden, Jess, after I'd told you she was a witch. She isn't really, you know. I just made it up."

"I knew that. I knew she wasn't a witch."

"How? I've always fooled you before. How did you know it wasn't true this time?"

"I asked the pigeons and they told me," Jessie replied.

Sitting waiting for the ambulance, she had heard them saying over and over again,

"No, not *true-ooo, not true-ooo*, no!"

"Pigeons can't talk, Jess," Alice protested, but Jessie just laughed.

"You don't know everything," she said.

The Bear

Stephen Elboz

The Bear

Stephen Elboz

It's no fun being grounded, especially when it's not your fault. I mean, I admit I kicked the football: but how was I to know the wind would change and make it swing round like that? Anyway, I've always said it was a stupid place to put a greenhouse.

After Dad had stopped jumping up and down, he said, "Joe, why is it you always attract trouble? What you need is something to keep you out of mischief." That was when Mum remembered the card in the newsagent's window. It seemed Mrs Pendergast, at the big house, wanted someone to keep her visiting grandson amused.

Dad's eyes positively lit up when he discovered she was prepared to pay and he telephoned with indecent haste so that everything was arranged.

That afternoon I found myself walking up to the big house. You had to go through these stone gates with an eagle on either side; behind them was a drive lined with trees. It was really long. Serves 'em right, I thought, if I fall down exhausted at the end. Mrs Pendergast would prob'ly have to give me my money and send me home again. Well, that cheered me up no end and I began to whistle.

Then I saw the house with Mrs Pendergast waiting on the steps and didn't whistle any more. She was frowning like a bulldog that had swallowed a wasp.

"You're late!" she boomed at me – like it was my fault her house was so far from the road.

"Come in," she said coldly, "and try not to touch anything."

Without another word I followed her into the hallway. Well, talk about grand. It had more pillars than a wedding cake. Then Mrs Pendergast went into a room where the furniture had golden tassels and in the cabinets were lots of china things my mum would have killed for. Perched on one of the sofas was this little blond kid.

"This is my grandson, Simon," announced Mrs Pendergast proudly.

I was shocked. The kid looked about six years old – nearly half my age! – with these large puppy dog eyes. Too late I realised the bitter truth. Dad had sold me into slavery as a *babysitter* to pay for his rotten greenhouse.

The kid climbed down off the sofa, came over and held out a pink mitt. He actually wanted me to shake hands!

"Pleased to meet you, Joe," he said – and do you know I think he really meant it.

"Splendid!" cooed ol' Mrs Pendergast. "Play nicely together and there'll be jelly and ice cream for tea."

I turned my look of injured pride on her, only to find she had already swept from the room.

"I'm glad you've arrived, Joe," the kid was saying. "Now we can start the bear hunt."

Bear hunt! I ask you. Was everyone here completely mad? I gazed at the kid pityingly and decided to let him down gently.

"As it happens, there are no bears in England," I informed him with all the authority of my age. "Least ways no bears you can hunt."

At this the kid got all excited – as if I'd taken his rattle away or something. "There are! There are!" he shouted, dancing about as though his feet were on fire and he was trying to stamp them out. "One sleeps on my bed every night and brings me my breakfast in the morning. He lives here with my grandma."

Coolly I fixed him eye to eye. "Oh yeah," I said. "Show me."

To give the kid credit he didn't back down. He just hared out into the hallway and up the stairs. At first I strolled casually after him, but thinking I might lose him, I began to run.

On the second landing I saw a door swing to.

Now I don't mind admitting that at this stage I was getting a tiny bit worried. The kid was so sure of himself and the house was certainly big enough for a bear. I mean it was not entirely impossible. Robert Griggs kept a snake in his bedroom for a whole month before his mum found it. Hesitantly I turned the door handle.

"Simon!" I hissed through the gap.

Catching my own reflection in a flaking dressing-table mirror I smiled with relief, seeing just an ordinary bedroom. Definitely not a bear's cage I decided. But where had the kid gone?

Something inside the wardrobe moved. I crept up, turned the brass latch and –

"RRRRRRRRRRRRR!"

A great, dark creature pounced on me. I was at the door, halfway out when I heard laughing.

Blood boiling mad I spun round. The kid was jumping up and down on the bed, his gran's dressing-gown slowly peeling off his shoulders and a fox fur sliding off his head. I felt pretty stupid, I can tell you. I mean he's just a kid and I'm years older than he is and have things like swimming certificates and a penknife with eight blades.

"That's . . . that's not funny, Simon," I said darkly. "It could have been dangerous. I mean, what if I had thought you were a real bear and gone and killed you?"

"Fo-oled you! Fo-oled you!" he chanted in his squeaky kid voice, all the time jumping up and down on the creaking bed. "You thought I was a be-ar!"

"For the last time," I said with forced patience, "there is no bear."

"He's hi-ding! He's hi-ding!"

"OK," I said. "I didn't want to tell you this, but I know somethin' far more fright'nin' than some stupid ol' bear."

Suddenly interested, the kid slithered off the bed and stood before me, lost in the over-sized dressing-gown.

"Oh? What?"

My brain was desperately trying to come up with something horrible enough to shock a little kid out of his socks. Five minutes later we stood in the bathroom. I pointed.

"The toilet?" said the kid throwing me a quizzical look.

"Course it's a toilet," I spluttered. Then I made my voice all mysterious. "What grown-ups never tell little kids like you is, that down every toilet lurks the bug-eyed King of the Underworld, protected by his army of vampire crocodiles."

"Wow," mouthed the kid, immediately jumping at the bait.

"Yeah. If the bug-eyed King of the Underworld doesn't like you he waits 'til you're sitting on the toilet, then he sends one of his vampire crocodiles through the pipes to bite you on the bum."

Pretty good, huh? I was just congratulating myself on the tale when I noticed this smile slowly creep across the kid's face.

"Oh, but not here," he piped up confidently. "My bear would frighten off your vampire crocodile."

"But they have jaws like this . . . and teeth like this . . . and claws like this . . ." I cried, gesturing like an idiot.

"My bear's even bigger and stronger," said the kid unimpressed.

Well this meant war. I was determined to scare him now. I mean, it had become a point of honour.

"Right, you asked for it," I said. "I'm going to tell you something no little kid should know, 'cause it's too dang'rous . . ." And narrowing my eyes I said, "To call the bug-eyed King of the Underworld himself, you must turn on the taps hard, then flush the toilet and blink your eyes quickly three times . . . and then, as you watch, this green, slimy hand rises up out of the toilet . . . and it'll be *him*."

"Do it then," sneered the kid. "I wouldn't be scared. My bear will protect me."

By now I half believed my story myself. I yanked on the bath taps, flushed the toilet and began blinking like some idiot in need of a pair of glasses.

The kid folded his arms, half amused by my antics. Slowly the filling cistern fizzled into silence, and nothing was happening.

"Told you so," said the kid triumphantly. "I told you your bug-eyed King of the Underworld is a scaredy cat."

But I wasn't listening. I had something else to worry about. The taps . . . they wouldn't turn off.

"Oh," said the kid all innocent like. "I should have warned you. If you turn the taps full on, they get stuck."

Worriedly I noticed that the water was rising faster than it could empty away. The kid jumped up and down clapping his hands in delight.

I thought his gran ought to be pleased by just how well I was keeping him amused. Perhaps she'd pay me double . . . only when I went to find her, I couldn't open the door.

"You shouldn't have locked it, Joe," I heard the kid whisper over my shoulder. "Last time the key got stuck, a man had to climb up a ladder to rescue me. That was fun." The kid sounded so cheerful I could have flushed him down the toilet, blond curls and all.

Was it my fault nothing in this ol' house worked prop'ly? I mean, it wasn't as if there were warning signs or anything. I rushed back and pulled on the taps as hard as I could, but the water still kept gushing out.

"If my bear was here he'd be strong enough to turn them off," said the kid.

"For once and for all there is no—" I straightened up so quickly that I cracked my head on some shelves. I mean, what a stupid place to put them.

Just before I staggered back and fell down, I had time to see the whole lot come away from the wall sending about a million bottles of expensive bubble bath smashing into the water. And, as I sat rubbing my head, wond'ring what kind of maniac needs so much bubble bath, I felt something splatter onto me. I didn't have to look to know the bath was overflowing.

The kid and me watched with horrified fascination. First the water dripped. Then it trickled. Then it cascaded over the bath's side.

The kid giggled. "This is fun, Joe," he said,

like I had deliberately planned it. "And just look at those lovely bubbles."

"Oh no," I groaned as the foam began to grow like something in a science fiction movie. For a moment the kid was overwhelmed by it. I dragged him free and he glared up at me like some angry dwarf with a white foam beard.

Just then a piercing scream told me that Mrs Pendergast had noticed the water dripping through her ceiling. She came battering on the door, blaming *me* for everything.

"What have you done to my poor, dear Simon, you wicked boy?" she bellowed.

Poor, dear Simon, I want it known, was happily splashing about in the now ankle deep water. I mean, I was only keeping him amused like I was supposed to do. She should have been pleased.

"You'll not get away with this!" threatened Mrs Pendergast storming off.

Soon me and the kid found ourselves pinned to the furthest wall by a crazy, quivering mass of suds. The kid remained remarkably cheerful about it.

"Don't worry," I whispered in a tough, big

brother kind of way to reassure him.

"Oh I'm not worried," he beamed. "My bear will rescue us."

"Listen – shud-up about your stupid bear," I said bitterly. "If I hear one more time about —" Suddenly my jaw went slack in disbelief. Behind all those trillions of bubbles a dark, menacing shape had appeared and was fighting to break through. It growled angrily as its foot plunged into the bath water.

"See," smiled the kid. "I told you my bear would come."

"That isn't a bear," I gasped.

"You mean . . . it's the bug-eyed King of the Underworld?"

"No . . . a million times worse than either of 'em."

Suddenly the figure clawed itself free of the bubbles.

The kid clutched me. My throat went dry. Hands were reaching out to grab me.

"But Dad," I cried. "It wasn't my fault!"

The Cowboy of
Paradise Farm

Elizabeth Laird

The Cowboy of Paradise Farm

Elizabeth Laird

One bright morning at Paradise Farm, Stewart Harvey, the farmer's son, came crashing down the stairs and into the kitchen. He looked at the clock. Ten minutes to nine already! Quickly, he tipped some cornflakes into his bowl, sploshed some milk over them and began to cram them into his mouth.

"You'll choke," warned his mum.

Stewart picked up his lunchbox.

"So long, partners. I gotta get out of town," he said, and dashed towards the door.

"You'd better run through the field," his dad called after him, "but don't forget to shut the gate behind you."

Stewart raced across the farmyard and wriggled under the fence into the cows' field.

"Hi there, Myrtle," he sang out to his favourite cow.

Myrtle mooed softly. She was used to Stewart. Her sisters, Ivy, Dewdrop, Petunia, Betty and Bandy-legs mooed too. They always did what Myrtle did.

Pottingdean Primary School was right next to Paradise Farm, just beyond the hedge at the bottom of the cows' field.

Stewart bounded down towards the gate that led into the playground. The bell had stopped ringing, and the children were quickly disappearing through the double doors that led into the cloakroom.

Stewart reached the gate, unlatched it, darted through and let it clang shut behind him. He began to race across the playground, but then he hesitated. The gate sounded as if it had shut. It looked as if it was shut. It must be shut, he thought. He ran into the school, after all his friends.

The morning ticked peacefully by. Up at the farm, Mrs Harvey was feeding the hens. Down in Pottingdean School, Miss Hackett, the headteacher, was writing lists in her office. In Mr Speckle's class, Stewart and all his friends were making a wildlife mural.

But up in the cows' field, something unusual was happening. Myrtle had pushed her pink wet nose against the gate at the bottom of her field, and it had swung wide, wide open.

"Maroomph!" snorted Myrtle joyfully, for she was a cow that loved adventures. Briskly, she trotted into the playground of Pottingdean School, and Ivy, Dewdrop, Petunia, Betty and Bandy-legs all trotted after her.

Meanwhile, in Mr Speckle's class the wildlife mural was coming along beautifully. Acres of painted green paper lay drying on the tables, and everyone was drawing rabbits, voles, shrews, hares, crows, skylarks, kestrels, dandelions, clover, thistles, spiders and worms to stick on it.

Stewart was absent-mindedly drawing a prickly cactus instead of the rabbit he was supposed to be doing, when he looked up and saw Myrtle's face pressed against the window.

"Waah!" he yelled, not because he was scared of Myrtle, but because he was surprised.

Mr Speckle jumped, and his glasses, which he always wore balanced on the end of his nose, fell off.

"Stewart," he said crossly, "don't shriek like that!"

"But sir . . ." began Stewart.

"That's *enough*!" said Mr Speckle, and he bent down and started groping about on the floor, looking for his glasses.

By now, everyone except for Mr Speckle had seen the cow too, only by this time there was not one, but six. Myrtle, Ivy, Dewdrop, Petunia, Betty and Bandy-legs were all trotting past the window. Chaos broke out.

"Oh look, sir. Cows!"

"There's hundreds and hundreds of them."

"Bet they're going to attack the school."

"Bet they're going to attack Miss Hackett's office."

"Bet they're going to attack Miss Hackett."

Mr Speckle was still hunting for his glasses.

The girls were trying to be helpful.

"I think I trod on them just now, sir. I heard a kind of crunching noise."

"You can borrow mine if you like, sir."

"You might see better if you sort of screw your eyes up, like this, sir."

At last, Mr Speckle found his glasses. They were cracked. He stood up, extremely annoyed.

"Be quiet!" he barked. "Sit down!"

The class subsided.

"Now then," said Mr Speckle, putting his broken glasses into his pocket. "What on earth was all that about?"

Mohinder got in first.

"In the playground, sir," he said, pointing out of the window. "Look. Loads and loads of cows."

Mr Speckle swivelled his head round to look.

There was not a cow to be seen. Myrtle, Ivy, Dewdrop, Petunia, Betty and Bandy-legs had just trotted on round the corner of the school.

"What nonsense," said Mr Speckle. "Now settle down, everyone, and get on quietly with your work," but with a puzzled frown, he opened the door that led directly from the classroom into the playground, and went outside.

Mr Speckle was too late. Myrtle had seen a pair of doors. They were all scratched and bashed, just like the doors leading into the friendly old milking parlour up at the farm, and she had butted them open and hurtled right in, followed, of course, by Ivy, Dewdrop, Petunia, Betty and Bandy-legs.

To their surprise, instead of being in their milking parlour, the cows found themselves in a corridor lined with pegs from which hung brightly coloured coats and bags.

They looked around for a moment, not knowing what to do. Petunia took a bite out of Linda Miles' shoebag. Dewdrop sniffed at Lucy Fairhead's lunchbox. Bandy-legs nibbled at Mohinder's coat and left a silvery stream of slobber down the sleeve.

But Myrtle was made of sterner stuff. She ignored the coats and the bags, and trotting down the corridor, barged straight into Mr Speckle's classroom, and Ivy, Dewdrop, Petunia, Betty and Bandy-legs barged in after her.

There was a moment of total silence while

everyone froze in horror. Then there was a
riot.

Lucy Fairhead screamed. Mohinder sat
down in the tray of paints. Linda Miles
practically fainted.

Stewart shook his head in disbelief.

"Myrtle!" he said. "And Ivy, Dewdrop,
Petunia, Betty and Bandy-legs! How on *earth*
did you get in here?"

The deafening sound of Mr Speckle's class
in hysterics made the cows panic. They
started charging round the room. Petunia

knocked Mr Speckle's desk over. Betty sat down on the nature display. Bandy-legs licked the mural. Stewart slid quietly up to Myrtle.

"Myrtle!" he cooed softly into her ear. "It's me, Stewart! Come with me, back to your nice field. The others will all follow you, Myrt. Be a leader – now!"

But the commotion had terrified Myrtle. She didn't even notice Stewart. She wheeled round and plunged out of the room, back into the corridor, and, of course, Ivy, Dewdrop, Petunia, Betty and Bandy-legs all plunged out after her, with Stewart in pursuit.

Mr Speckle, who had peered round the playground but had found nothing there, decided that his class had tricked him, and, very cross indeed, he went back inside at the very moment that the door leading out into the corridor shut behind Stewart and the cows. He looked at his devastated classroom in disbelief.

"What on *earth*'s been going on in here!" he roared.

Everyone was making so much noise they didn't even hear him.

"I'm going to fetch Miss Hackett at once,"

said Mr Speckle, and he marched out into the corridor.

Sitting in her office, still making lists, Miss Hackett was puzzled. The school was filled with strange sounds. Clatterings were coming from the kitchen. Boomings and tinklings could be heard in the percussion cupboard. There were crashes and thuds in every single classroom, along with the wild din of a hundred children shouting. She opened the door of her room and went out to see what was going on.

She walked along the corridor and looked into the hall where the tables were supposed to be laid out for dinner. It was as if a hurricane had swept through it. Benches were overturned, cutlery lay in drifts on the floor, and of the dinner ladies there was no sign.

Mystified, Miss Hackett turned round. What was that, disappearing round the corner at the end of the corridor? It looked like a long tail with a black tuft on the end. It looked as if it belonged to a ... Miss Hackett shut her eyes for a moment and opened them again. The thing, whatever it was, had disappeared.

"I must get my eyes tested," she thought.

A strange smell was coming from the library. It was a warm, farmyard, earthy kind of smell, like the smell of . . . Miss Hackett sniffed, and opened the library door.

There, on the carpet, was a huge blob of something brown and warm and moist. It steamed gently.

Miss Hackett bent over it and sniffed. Surely it wasn't a . . . It couldn't be a . . . Not right here, in Pottingdean School library!

Mr Speckle, finding Miss Hackett's office empty, had set off in search of her. He found her at last in the library. She was standing as if in a trance, looking down at the floor.

"Miss Hackett!" said Mr Speckle, waving his arms wildly, "my class has gone mad! Completely mad!"

Miss Hackett didn't answer. Mr Speckle stepped closer to her, and felt his foot squelch into something soft and mushy. He bent down to see what it was.

"I don't believe it!" he wailed. "I've trodden in a cowpat!"

Meanwhile the cows, who had been

exploring the staffroom and frightening the teachers into fits, were trotting back down the corridor towards Mr Speckle's classroom. They had had enough of this scary, noisy place and they wanted to go back to their nice quiet field. Myrtle, still in the lead, had calmed down and had noticed Stewart for the first time. He was tiptoeing along beside her, murmuring soothingly. "Come on, Myrtle! Good girl! Come home with me! You know you want to."

At that moment, Miss Hackett and Mr Speckle flung open the library door, and saw that the corridor was full of cows. They gasped in horror.

"Stewart!" roared Miss Hackett.

"Miss Hackett!" gasped Stewart.

"Moo!" bellowed Myrtle.

"Cows!" wailed Mr Speckle.

"Mr Speckle!" croaked Stewart.

They all stood and looked at each other.

"Stewart!" said Miss Hackett at last. "Where do all these cows come from?"

"They're Dad's," said Stewart. "The big one's Myrtle, and the others are called . . ."

"I don't want to know what their names are,"

hissed Miss Hackett. "What are they doing in Pottingdean School?"

"It's all right, Miss Hackett, I can explain everything," said Stewart, out of habit. Then he stopped. He couldn't explain anything. He had no idea what had happened. Suddenly, a nasty thought occurred to him. Perhaps on his way to school in the morning he hadn't shut the gate of the cows' field properly after all. He certainly didn't want to explain that. He shook his head. "Well no, actually, I'm afraid I can't explain," he said, "but don't worry. I'll get them out of here. Come on, Myrtle!"

To everyone's astonishment, Myrtle obediently dropped her head and mooing gently, she followed Stewart along the corridor, through the cloakroom, out of the double doors and into the playground, and Ivy, Dewdrop, Petunia, Betty and Bandy-legs trotted along after her.

Then, giving them friendly whacks on the rump, and with cries of "Yahoo!" and "Gid along there, sisters!" Stewart drove the cows across the playground and back into their nice quiet field. Very carefully, he shut the gate, then he sauntered back across the playground, waving his hand modestly to the entire school, who were watching him from every window and greeting his return with wild cheers.

You will be glad to know that this story had a happy ending, or rather, several happy endings. Myrtle, Ivy, Dewdrop, Petunia, Betty and Bandy-legs realised after all that home was best, and they never strayed out of their field again.

Mr Speckle didn't bother to get his glasses mended. He thought he'd wear contact lenses instead in future, to save the bother of having his glasses drop off the end of his nose.

Miss Hackett took early retirement. She decided that living in the country was too much of a strain, and she moved to a flat right in the middle of Manchester, where she was certain never to see a cow from one year's end to the next.

As for Stewart, when he grew up he went off to the Wild West and became a famous cowboy. And he never, ever, left a gate open again.

The Gift

Sharon Creech

The Gift

Sharon Creech

On my ninth birthday, when I opened my present from Gran, I could hardly believe my eyeballs.

I had saved her present for last because *usually* Gran gives me the most perfect gifts. Not expensive ones, but neat ones. I am her only grandson and she spoils me. Or at least she *used* to.

One year she gave me a chemistry set with

which I could bubble up all kinds of perfectly amazing and disgusting smelly things, and another year she gave me a magic kit from which I learned to snatch coins out of people's ears.

Gran's presents had always been the best, and always a surprise. You never knew what she would come up with. My parents wouldn't let me ask for specific things, anyway. They thought that was rude. They thought you should let the giver give whatever he or she wanted.

So I had no idea whatsoever what would be in that box from Gran. It was a smallish box, long and thin and flat, wrapped in plain blue paper and tied in white ribbon. It looked like the sort of box that a watch would come in: a special watch, an underwater watch that glows in the dark and has alarm bells and buzzers and tells the date. The sort of watch that if you fell off your bike and landed on your wrist, it wouldn't even break. The watch, I mean. Your wrist might break, but the watch wouldn't because it would be a super-indestructible, amazing, magnificent watch.

I slowly removed the paper. I could hardly

wait. It was going to be terrific. It was going to be unbelievable. I lifted the lid.

It wasn't terrific. But it *was* unbelievable. Unbelievably boring. Unbelievably stupid. Unbelievably the most awful, stupid, boring gift anyone had ever given me – ever – in my whole entire life.

It was a pencil.

You heard me right: a *pencil*. I turned the box upside down and shook it and examined it carefully, just in case there was a huge amount of money in there, or anything else – anything at all. Oh please, I thought, please let there be something else in this box so that I can look up at my Gran, who is sitting there watching me, and say thank you without letting her see that I am immensely and completely and totally disappointed to be unwrapping a stupid, boring pencil.

Poor old Gran, I was thinking. She has lost her poor old brains. What could she have been thinking of – giving me a *pencil*?

There was nothing else in the box. I turned the pencil around in my fingers. "Mm," I said, "what a nice pencil. What an interesting pencil. I can always use a pencil. A person can never have too many pencils, can they? A pencil is certainly a useful thing, isn't it? You can do so many different and interesting and useful things with it, can't you?"

I was lying.

I couldn't stop myself, though. On I went. "You can write with it and you can – you can, um, *draw* with it, yes, that's a good thing to do with a pencil, isn't it? Write and draw *too*. It's just amazing all the amazing and unbelievable things—"

My father interrupted me, thank goodness, or I would have been blathering on like that for a few years. "Let's have some cake," he said.

"Cake, yes! What a great idea!" I agreed.

For a while, I forgot about the pencil. To tell you the truth, I had put it back in its box and tossed it on my desk and soon it was buried under piles of magazines and school books and gum wrappers.

About a week later, when I had to write a report for school, I cleared off my desk, and that's when I found it again. I took it out of its box and examined it.

It was a seven-sided wooden pencil covered

in colourful printed paper: the sort of pencil you might expect the Queen to write with. No, on second thoughts, the Queen would probably have a gold pencil or at least a silver one.

The design on the pencil was of many-coloured leaves: red ones, blue ones, green ones, and tiny gold ones that shimmered in the light. One end of the pencil was sharpened into a black point and at the other end was a simple, pink rubber.

That's about it. At least it was sharp, and since I had a report to write, I thought I might as well use it. What the heck.

I wasn't too good at school things. Teachers were always on at me about my messy handwriting and my poor spelling and my "jumbled" thoughts. So I didn't much look forward to writing reports. This one was supposed to be about a true experience. Wow! There's a thrilling topic for you.

I figured I'd write about the time I accidentally exploded a jar of pickles with my chemistry set. I was in a hurry to write, because if I finished all my homework by eight o'clock I could watch television for an hour. I dashed something off and didn't even bother to re-read it. It was done. That was good enough for me. Time for television!

Three days later, the teacher handed back my report. Usually I didn't bother to read the comments in the margins. They always said the same things: "Watch your spelling!" "Poor handwriting!" "Can't read this?!" "Incomplete sentence!" On and on. At the end of the paper, the teacher usually wrote, "Try harder" or "Is this finished?"

As I stuffed this report in my binder, I noticed a word written in the margin: "Terrific!"

Maybe I got someone else's report back by mistake. I looked at the name at the top of the paper. It was my name alright. Rather neatly written, too, I noticed.

I glanced down the left side of the first page. The teacher had written: "Very good!" and "Nice handwriting!" and "I like this."

I checked the name at the top again. Still mine.

All over the paper were these amazing comments. At the end, the teacher had written: "Very well done. This is so true and honest!"

At home, I showed the report to my parents. Normally I don't show them anything unless they jump up and down and insist, because then they repeat the same things the teacher did: "You ought to try harder. Can't you write more neatly?" On and on.

When they read this report about the chemistry explosion, I noticed that they kept glancing back at the top of the first page, just as I had done, to be sure they were reading *my* paper.

"Well," my father said. "Well, well, well."

"Did *you* write this?" my mother said. "I mean, it's just so neat – and – *good*."

That night I had another written assignment: describe the life cycle of a frog. Another thrilling topic. As I sat there, trying to think how to begin, I noticed the pencil again. I turned it around in my hands. I sharpened it. I started to write.

The report was handed back the following week. "How creative!" the teacher had written. "How original!" and "Very neat!" and "Well done!"

I showed my parents.

"Well," my father said. "Well, well, well."

My mother looked at the name at the top. "*You* wrote this?"

But the next day, the teacher handed back another paper. It was one that I had written in class, in ink, and I had thought it was quite good.

It wasn't. In the margins, the teacher had written: "Sloppy handwriting" and "What does this mean?" and "Watch your spelling."

I didn't show that paper to my parents. I hid it in my desk.

I started to wonder about the pencil with its red and blue and green and gold leaves. I picked it up and turned it around in my fingers.

Could it be lucky? Was it magic? Did it have a brain of its own?

For the next month, I wrote absolutely everything with that pencil. Homework, classwork. Maths, Science, English. It was amazing. Teachers were falling all over themselves writing "Well done!" and "Good handwriting!" and "How true!" and "How creative!" On and on and on.

I kept that pencil with me at all times. I guarded it as if it were made of pure gold. If someone asked to borrow a pencil, I gave them one of my old yellow chewed ones. One time, the boy sitting next to me reached for my special pencil saying, "Let me use this a minute, okay?" and I snatched it back so fast he couldn't even blink. I reacted as if he'd tried to steal a hundred pounds from me. "What's your *problem*?" he said. I gave him one of my old yellow chewed pencils. "Nothing," I said. "Nothing."

I sharpened that pencil about five times a day. I wrote and wrote and wrote with it. It was definitely magic. It knew how to spell. It knew how to use big words. It had very neat handwriting.

I started getting worried when I noticed how short it was getting. Oh *no*, I thought. Oh *no*. What will I do when it's gone?

I had nightmares in which I'd be running through a forest looking for my pencil. I'd be sweating and screaming. "Where are you? Where are you?"

I tried to press lightly when I used it, hoping that the lead would not be used up so fast. I tried not to sharpen it until it was worn right down to the wood.

By now, only a few soiled and smudged leaves were left on the short stub of the pencil. But the pink rubber was still clean. I had never rubbed out a single word, that's how perfect the pencil was. That's how brilliant it was. It didn't make mistakes.

I started writing shorter papers. If a teacher asked for one page, I'd write half a page, figuring I could save my pencil that way. The teachers started writing things like, "Very good, but a bit short" and "Please write more."

In desperation, I called my Gran and asked her if she had another pencil like the one she had given me.

"Oh, did you like it then?" she asked.

"Like it? Of course I *like* it. It's the best, it's perfect, it's magic. But where did you get it? Where can I buy more?"

"Oh, you can't *buy* them," she said. Her grandmother had given her three of these pencils when Gran was my age. Gran had used one of them, just as I had. She had worn it down to a tiny stub. Then she had saved the other two. "One of them I gave to you," she said.

"And the other one?" I asked. "There's one more? Where is it? Can I have it? I *must* have it. I've *got* to have it."

The next day she brought me the last flowered pencil. It was in a box, wrapped in blue paper, with white ribbon. She didn't say anything. She just handed me the box, and gave me a funny look.

That night I examined my short, worn-out pencil. There was about two inches left. Maybe I could discover what made it special. Then maybe I could make my own, and I would never run out.

I took one of my old yellow chewed pencils and a knife, and slit the yellow pencil down one side. Inside was a thin piece of lead surrounded by wood. Then I took my worn-out pencil with its coloured-leaved paper. I slit it down one side. Inside it looked the same as the yellow one: a thin piece of lead surrounded by wood. I held the two pieces of lead side by side. They looked the same. They felt the same. They even smelled the same.

As I put the lead back inside the coloured-leaved pencil, my hands shook, and the lead broke. I slid the two pieces of lead in, end to end, and closed the wood around it. I taped the pencil round and round, but when I tried to write with it, the lead wobbled.

It wouldn't work.

That night my assignment was to write a story about generosity. I used an old yellow pencil. I wrote *very* slowly. I even checked the dictionary to be sure I was spelling correctly. When I needed to rub out words, which was a lot, I used the rubber on the end of my worn-out coloured-leaved pencil.

I wrote about my grandmother's gift: the magic pencil.

At the end of the story, I said that she had given me one more pencil, her last one. It was in a flat box, wrapped in blue paper with white ribbon. I said that I wouldn't use it. I would keep it. Maybe some day I would have a grandson and on his birthday, I would give it to him.

I haven't got that assignment back yet. I wonder how I did.

The Mysterious Meadow

Joan Aiken

The Mysterious
Meadow

Joan Aiken

Old Mrs Lazarus had died, aged ninety-four.
For the last sixty years she had owned Fox
Hill Farm, up above Highbury Village. Now
her family had all come together – or most of
them – to attend her funeral, to hear her Will
read, and to learn what was to become of the
property. Fox Hill Farm covered several

hundred acres, over the slope of Highbury Hill, and any estate so close to London was now very valuable indeed.

"It's a wonder she hung on to it for so long," big fat Saul Wodge, one of the grandsons over from Chicago, was saying to his cousin Mark Briskitt, a professor from Manchester. Saul owned nine Fun Parks, scattered all over America, and was about to open a tenth.

"Granny Lazarus grew wonderful crops – parsley, basil, sunflower seeds. She and Uncle Tod were into organic farming long ago, before the rest of the country had even heard of it. They were selling to big hotels and supermarkets."

"No wonder she wanted to be buried under a tree."

"*Very* peculiar – not very nice at all!" said Petunia Wodge, Saul's wife. "Buried under a *tree*? What kind of interment is *that*, I ask you?"

The ceremony had taken place under a young beech tree, one of a narrow belt of beeches forming a windbreak between a ploughed field and a piece of rough downland pasture which stretched alongside Highbury Common.

Little Rickie Wodge, youngest son of the great-great-grandchildren, had already found blackberries scattered over the brambles bordering the Common, and his cheeks were stained purple.

"*Rickie*! Come back out of that! What ever have you found? You'll poison yourself!"

Rickie's mother Lara was in Chicago, nursing his six-week-old sister. Petunia, Rickie's grandmother, took off after him like a fury, but she wore shiny black shoes with three-inch heels and a tight lavender-coloured skirt; there was no possible way she could catch up with him as he bounded about, faster than a fire-cracker, fizzing with glee. Brought up in an apartment on the twenty-first floor, he had never seen so much grass in his life.

Forty grown-up children were discussing the Will. Sarah Lazarus had lived so long that her three sons and two daughters had died before her.

"*Two acres* to each grandchild! Of their own choice! How in the name of reason is that ever going to be sorted out? It will need half a dozen computers. And how are we going to find everybody?"

One of Sarah's sons, Luke, had moved to Buenos Aires and had six children. None of these had turned up at the funeral.

"It's going to take twenty years to settle the question of who owns every different bit," groaned Titus, the eldest son of Tod Lazarus. "And, in the meantime, here's the Department of Transport wanting to run a bypass road across the hill, and Moko Supermarkets anxious to build a Superstore . . ."

Furiously he stamped on a beech-nut which a nervous squirrel had dropped from a branch overhead. Golden leaves were beginning to flutter down from the beeches.

The September sun shone warmly on the descendants of Sarah Lazarus as they paced about indignantly, reading copies of their grandmother's Will.

"And what about this clause? Titania's Piece? Which field is that, anyway?"

"It's the strip of pasture-land beyond the beech trees," Mark Briskitt told his cousin Dinsie from Florida.

"What does Great-grandma mean when she says she is leaving it to the Travellers? Who are the Travellers, in mercy's name?"

"Travellers are gypsies. Egyptians, they used to be called. I think they have always used this piece as a camp-ground, right back to the Middle Ages. I can remember when I was a boy," said Mark, "and I used to come here for holidays, quite often there would be half-a-dozen horse-drawn wagons up there. Once an old lady called Mrs Lee told my fortune."

All of a sudden he looked wistful, remembering those days.

"She ever say you'd make a million?" big fat Saul Wodge asked with a guffaw.

"No . . . She said I'd come to the brink and step back from it. I often wondered what she meant . . ."

"But how could Great-grandma Lazarus leave Titania's Piece to the Travellers? Who *are* they? Do they have any legal rights?"

"Some of the local people round here say that piece of land always has belonged to them." Truda, the wife of Titus, a thin dark girl, spoke hesitatingly.

"How could they ever prove that?" snapped Petunia Wodge.

"It's said there's a boggle-patch on that bit of land."

"And what," demanded Cousin Kent Lazurus from Poughkeepsie, "what, pray, is a boggle-patch?"

"It's an area of land surface that actually lies in another dimension. Belongs to other powers, you might say. So if you tread on it, for instance, you disappear," explained Mark, who was a professor of mathematics.

"Is that so?" demanded Saul Wodge, laughing even more heartily. "So, I just have to hike across that patch of pasture a few times, and I'll vanish clean away? Say! That would be a really *great* idea for a Fun Park. Let's give it a try!"

He strode off through the belt of trees to the rough downland turf beyond, and began methodically pacing backwards and forwards across it.

"Hey, Mark! How *big* is this alleged bogey-patch – or whatever you call it?" he shouted.

"Only about as big as a dinner-plate," Tansy, Mark's wife told him. She glanced about for her eight-year-old daughter. "Tish! Run and find your cousin Rickie and bring him down to the farmhouse for tea. It's time we were on our way."

Slowly all the cousins and second-cousins and their wives and children began to trickle away, leaving the high warm hillside where fallen leaves lay on thin, fine grass.

Voices floated back in gusts on the afternoon breeze.

"Shame to break up the estate, really . . ."

"A highway *and* a supermarket though — we'd all be millionaires . . ."

"But where can the Travellers be found? Do they have a legal address? Do they have a *lawyer*?"

"Who is Titania when she's at home?"

The sun slipped round the side of the hill. Dusk was beginning to creep into corners, under blackberry bushes, between the high straight trunks of beech trees.

Tish Briskitt and her cousin Rickie had found a hollow tree and made themselves a house in it.

Cousin Saul Wodge, red-faced and spluttering with laughter, still paced pertinaciously back and forth across the strip of grassland.

"Hey, watch me, fellas! I've just about covered it all, now!"

Nobody was paying much attention to him any more, except the two children, watching from their tree-house, and Cousin Mark from Manchester.

Tish's mother Tansy called the children again.

"Tish! Rickie! Will you come along now!"

But Rickie was wilful and made off, giggling and shrieking, in the opposite direction, after his grandfather Saul.

"Grandpa! Wait for me!"

"I'll catch Rickie!" shouted Tish. "I'll collar him, Mum! You'll see!"

Off she darted after Rickie, her black plaits flying out behind her.

Then they all saw big fat Saul suddenly vanish, like a match-flame blown out, like a thin sheet of glass turned sideways on.

"*Hey, fellas!*" he was calling, but his voice died away faintly on the wind.

Rickie, scudding after him, vanished in exactly the same way, two seconds later.

"*Mark*! NO!" shouted Mark's wife, rigid with

horror, at the edge of the meadowland.

Mark, halfway across the grass in pursuit of his young cousin, pulled up and stood still.

So did his daughter Tish, just behind him.

"Dad!" she wailed. "Where's Rickie gone? Where is Uncle Saul?"

Husband, wife, daughter, looked at one another for a long, long minute, in complete silence. Then, still silent, taking hands, holding tight on to one another, they began to walk down to the farm, away from Titania's Piece.

The sun slipped behind the hill.